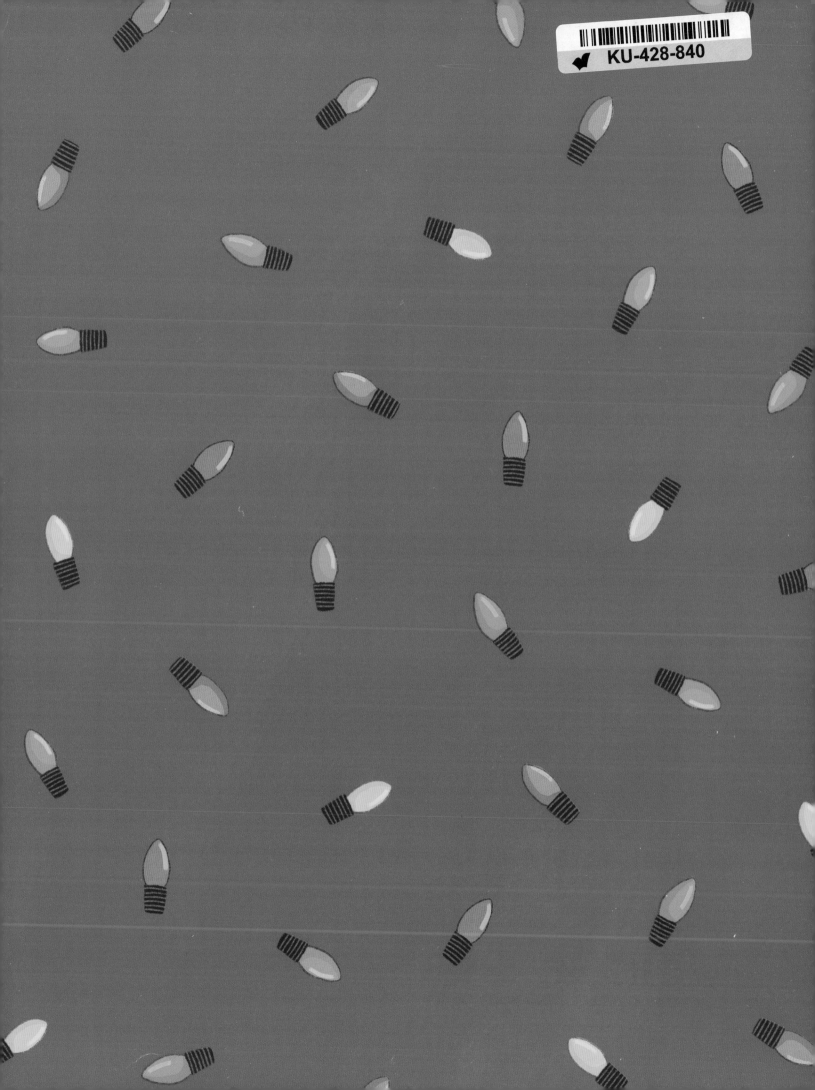

First published 2023 by Nosy Crow Ltd
Wheat Wharf, 27a Shad Thames
London, SE1 2XZ, UK

Nosy Crow Eireann Ltd,
44 Orchard Grove, Kenmare,
Co Kerry, V93 FY22, Ireland

www.nosycrow.com

ISBN 978 1 80513 291 2

Printed in Poland.
Papers used by Nosy Crow are made from wood grown in sustainable forests.
1 3 5 7 9 8 6 4 2

Written by Lucy Feather Illustrated by Christine Cuddihy

SNAPPER

The Perfect Christmas Tree

nosy crow

JOHN LEWIS
& PARTNERS

Though Alfie didn't like to shop,
today he didn't mind.
The market sold all sorts of things.
Who knew what he would find?

"Oh, look! What's this?" he wondered.
"Grow a perfect Christmas tree?
Could I grow my very own?
How **brilliant** that would be!"

Back home, he asked his nan
how he might plant the little seed.
"A pot, some earth and water.
Yes, I think that's all you'll need.

But please, my love,
remember that a tree
takes time to grow."

Still Alfie watched and waited –
and it did seem **very** slow!

He waited and he waited –
he just didn't want to sleep . . .

And then, when it was morning,
he rushed down to take a peep.

There it was – **at last!** –
a little shoot all new and green.
He thought it was the most
exciting thing he'd **ever** seen.

And from that moment onwards, it grew more

and more

and **MORE**,

until it suddenly looked very **different** from before.

With shiny leaves and smiley mouth
– a little tickle trap –
it nibbled Alfie's fingers
and then closed up with a **snap!**

Next day, when Alfie ran downstairs,
he saw to his delight,
his happy, snappy friend had grown
much bigger in the night!

"Everyone, meet Snapper –
and I'm sure you'll all agree
that Snapper is an absolutely
perfect **Christmas tree!**

Come on, Snapper, we can show them
you're just like the rest.
Stand up straight, just like a tree.
Please, Snapper, try your best . . .

Oh dear – that didn't go to plan,
now Poppy's in a flap!
But, wait! I know a way that
we can use your friendly snap . . .

Let's make a paper garland!
Come on, Snapper, take a bite."

But Mum said, "Alfie,
are you sure?
It doesn't look quite right!"

That night the family woke up –
what **was** that funny sound?
A gentle creaking, stretching noise
as something moved around.

Alfie stared in wonder –
"But you used to be so small . . ."
Yes, it was **Snapper!**
He had **grown**, and now
he was **so** tall!

"I'm sorry, Alfie," Mum said, as she slowly shook her head.
"Perhaps it would be better if . . . he lived outside instead."

When morning came,
poor Snapper shivered in the chilly snow.
Our not-so-happy, snappy friend
had nowhere else to go.

Now, Snapper knew full well
he was no ordinary tree.
If **only** they would listen –
he just wished that they could see.

That night, the "real" tree was lit,
and Snapper looked inside.
He gazed in at the love and warmth,
then hung his head and sighed.

And at that very moment,
Alfie looked at Snapper too.
He stared into the dark and
wished he knew what he should do.

Alfie trudged upstairs to bed
and all that long, **sad** night,
he thought about his snappy friend
and how to put things **right**.

By Christmas morning,
Alfie knew **exactly** what to do.
He slipped his coat and boots on
and a cosy beanie too.

He paused to take a present
and stepped out into the snow.
His family were puzzled
as they quietly watched him go.

Then Alfie put the present down
and **hugged** his best friend tight.

"Happy Christmas, Snapper!
Everything will be all right."

And as the family all joined them
on that snowy day,
"Ahem," Mum cleared her throat,
"there's something I would like
to say . . .

Thank you both for showing us
how Christmas ought to be.
Snapper, please forgive us.
Welcome to our family!"

"Oh, thank you, Mum!" said Alfie.
"Please can Snapper **really** stay?"

Then Snapper suddenly went . . .

SNAP!
and snatched the gifts away!

But as they watched and waited there,
it soon became quite clear
that Alfie's special Christmas tree
had had a bright idea . . .

For only **certain** Christmas trees

can **unwrap** presents too,

and clever, helpful Snapper

showed them ALL
that he could do!

And everyone (and Poppy too!)
was happy to agree
that Snapper was an absolutely
perfect Christmas tree!

A Christmas can be what you like,
as everyone must know,
so make your Christmas yours alone –
let your traditions **grow**.

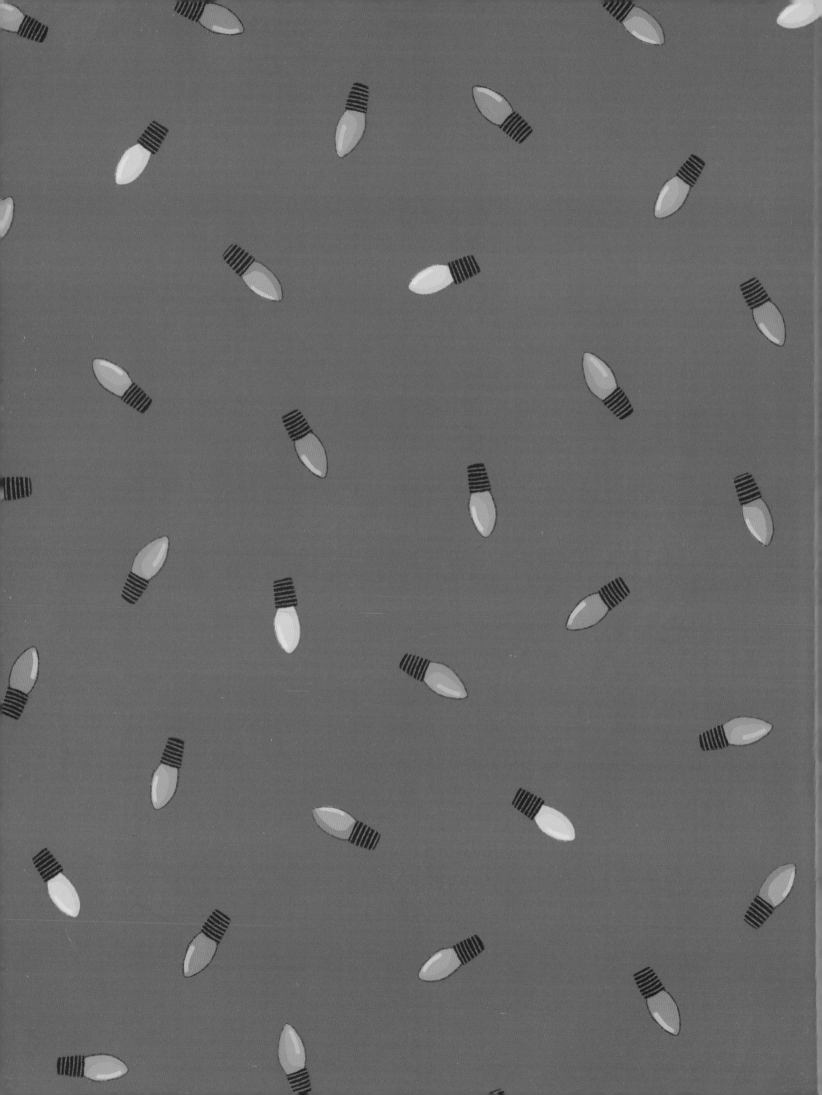